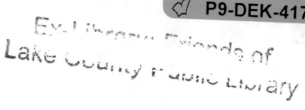

Jason and the Aliens Down the Street

Jason and the Aliens Down the Street

by **Gery Greer** and **Bob Ruddick**
Illustrations by **Blanche L. Sims**

HarperCollins*Publishers*

Other books by Gery Greer and Bob Ruddick

Let Me Off This Spaceship!

Max and Me and the Time Machine

American Bookseller Pick of the List 1983
School Library Journal Best Book of 1983
Master List for Dorothy Canfield Fisher Children's Book Award
Nominated for Northwest Library Association Young Readers Choice Award 19

Max and Me and the Wild West

This Island Isn't Big Enough for the Four of Us!

South Dakota Prairie Pasque Children's Book Award Winner 1990
Utah Children's Literature Award 1990

Jason and the Aliens Down the Street
Text copyright © 1991 by Gery Greer and Bob Ruddick
Illustrations copyright © 1991 by Blanche L. Sims
Printed in the United States of America. For information address
HarperCollins Children's Books, a division of HarperCollins Publishers,
10 East 53rd Street, New York, NY 10022.
1   2   3   4   5   6   7   8   9   10
First Edition

Library of Congress Cataloging-in-Publication Data
Greer, Gery.
    Jason and the aliens down the street / Gery Greer and Bob Ruddick;
illustrations by Blanche L. Sims.
        p.   cm.
    Summary: Jason meets Cooper Vor and Lootna, aliens from space now
living on Earth, and travels with them to a distant planet in an
attempt to retrieve a stolen energy crystal.
    ISBN 0-06-021761-8. — ISBN 0-06-021762-6 (lib. bdg.)
    [1. Science fiction.   2. Extraterrestrial beings—Fiction.
3. Adventure and adventurers—Fiction.]   I. Ruddick, Bob.
II. Sims, Blanche, ill.   III. Title.
PZ7.G85347Jas   1991   90-47386
[Fic]—dc20   CIP
                                                                AC

To Michelle

one

"Stop that, Ranger!" I yelled. "I'm not kidding! Cut it out!"

It was a sunny summer morning and I was in my backyard. I was trying to train Ranger to do tricks. Ranger was the dog I had borrowed from my neighbor, Mrs. Pelico.

I was beginning to think I had borrowed the wrong dog.

"I've just about had it with you, Ranger!" I yelled. "Let go of my pants leg or else!"

Training Ranger was part of my latest money-making project. My plan was simple. First I would teach Ranger to do some really neat tricks. And then I would become a door-to-door dog trainer.

I would take Ranger and go around the neighborhood ringing doorbells. I'd offer to train people's dogs—for a fee, of course. After people saw the terrific things Ranger could do, they wouldn't be able to stop themselves. They'd hire me right away.

"Okay, *now* look what you've done!" I said. "You've gone and ripped my jeans. Are you happy? Are you satisfied?"

Ranger *was* happy. He *was* satisfied. He went bounding around the yard in big circles, woofing.

I shook my head and sighed.

I was training Ranger with a book I'd checked out of the library. It was called *Good Dog!* and it told how to train your dog in seven easy days. Whoever wrote the book definitely didn't know Ranger. I'd been working with him for three days, and so far his best trick was knocking me over and standing on my chest.

Finally Ranger came charging back and sat down in front of me, wagging his tail.

I glared at him. I wanted him to know I meant business.

"All right, Ranger," I said sternly. "I *hope* we're ready to settle down. Are we ready to settle down?"

He wagged his tail some more.

"Good," I said. "I'm very glad to hear it. Okay, Ranger, I'll tell you what. Let's work on our fetching."

I took a rubber ball out of my pocket. Ranger thought that was pretty exciting. He jumped to his feet and wiggled his rear end.

"Okay, big fella," I said, cocking my arm. *"Fetch!"*

I threw the ball across the yard. Ranger took off like a shot, kicking up grass.

He caught up with the ball. He *passed* the ball. He snatched up my father's fishing hat from a lawn chair and kept on running!

He disappeared through the bushes into the next yard.

"Ranger!" I yelled. *"Come back here!"*

I broke into a run. I couldn't lose that fishing hat. My father loved that fishing hat.

I chased Ranger at top speed. After three backyards he was still going strong. At this rate he was going to fetch that hat all the way to China.

I raced through a sprinkler. I leaped over a sandbox. I squeezed through a hedge into the fourth backyard.

And stopped short.

There was Ranger. Just standing there. Frozen. He was staring at something in the middle of the yard. His mouth was hanging open, and the fishing hat was lying on the grass in front of him.

I looked over where he was looking.

It was a cat. Sitting there calmly. A silky black cat.

Or *was* it? . . .

There was something weird about it. It was too tall, for one thing. And its tail was too long, almost like a monkey's. And those ears—they belonged on a rabbit! They were about a foot long!

Whatever it was, it was watching me with its glowing purple eyes. I had the

feeling it was smiling.

My skin began to prickle.

Suddenly, the creature moved.

With a smooth, lazy motion it reached around with its tail and picked up a cup. It lifted the cup to its mouth and took a sip.

Then it turned its purple eyes on Ranger. It gave a single short growl.

At least I thought it was a growl. Actually, it sounded more like a word.

What it sounded like was: "Boo!"

two

Ranger didn't like being spoken to by a cat. He gave a loud yelp and dived back through the hedge. I could hear him galloping toward home.

I was alone. With the cat. If it *was* a cat. Maybe it was a man-eating rabbit.

I felt like galloping home myself. But first I had to get that fishing hat back. My father would never forgive me if I lost it.

The creature was watching my every move. I began to edge toward the hat. "Nice kitty," I said.

Slowly I leaned down toward the hat.

I reached out until I—

"Hi, there!" came a voice from the house.

I almost fell over.

A man pushed open the screen door and came down the back steps. He had a friendly face, a deep tan, and a lot of muscles.

"Don't pay any attention to Lootna," he said with a grin. "She's a little strange, but she's harmless."

I picked up my father's hat, stuck it in my pocket, and tried to look normal. "Oh?" I said. "I, er, I mean, is she some kind of cat?"

"She's a Ganxian," said the man. "She's smarter than a cat—and a lot more trouble, too. Like I said, she's a little strange."

The creature glared at the man. Then

it raised its nose in the air. "Hmmpf," it said.

I stared at it. Hmmpf? Did it say "Hmmpf"?

"By the way, the name's Cooper Vor," said the man. "My friends call me Coop. You from around here?"

"Yeah. I'm Jason Harkness," I said. "I live down that way about four houses."

I thought maybe I should explain to Mr. Vor what I was doing in his back-yard. So I told him about Ranger and my door-to-door dog-training idea.

When I finished, Mr. Vor looked at me with admiration. "Now that's original thinking, kid!" he said. "A door-to-door dog trainer, huh? I can see you're a real idea man."

"Well, I don't know . . ." I said. "I mean, Ranger hasn't really learned any tricks. All he did was run away with my father's hat. Then he got scared when he saw Lootna, and he ran home."

"I noticed *you* didn't run home. You stood your ground."

"Well—"

"That took guts, kid," said Mr. Vor. "Real guts. I mean, just look at Lootna. She's twice the size of a cat and has ears like canoe paddles. She's enough to make anyone run for cover."

Lootna didn't seem to like the remark about her ears. She gave Mr. Vor a hard look and made a "Pffft!" sound.

"Actually, I *was* a little scared," I admitted.

"Don't be modest, Jason," said Mr. Vor. He gave me a friendly whack on the shoulder. "I can see you've got spunk. Nerve. Backbone. I tell you what. How

would you like a job?"

"A job?"

"Sure, a part-time job. As my assistant."

"Well . . ." I said.

My mind was racing. Actually, it looked like my dog-training business was in real trouble. So a job would be nice. On the other hand . . .

"By the way, you're not afraid of heights, are you?" Mr. Vor asked. "Or high speeds?"

I blinked. "Uh, no, I guess not," I said.

"And are you pretty fast on your feet? I mean, when there's danger around?"

"Uh, well, yes, I guess so," I said.

"And how are you in situations of zero gravity?"

"Zero gravity?"

"Never mind. I'm sure you'd do fine. Okay, now here's the scoop, Jason. I need an assistant. You're a little younger than I had in mind, but I'm willing to give you a try. If you do a good job, I'll hire you permanently. What do you say?"

I was totally confused. What kind of job was he talking about?

"Uh, Mr. Vor—"

"Call me Coop."

"Uh, Coop, just what sort of work do you do?"

Coop shifted his weight.

"Before I tell you that," he said, "I have to tell you a secret. Can you keep a secret?"

I nodded.

"Good," said Coop. "I'm an alien from outer space. Lootna is too, of course."

three

I stared at Coop. Obviously the guy was bonkers. I mean, he didn't *look* bonkers, but obviously he *was* bonkers.

I tried to smile. "Heh, heh," I said. "An alien from outer space, huh? That's a good one."

Suddenly the cat creature cleared her throat. She was looking at Coop with her eyebrows raised.

"*Well,*" she said in a perfectly clear voice, "I *suppose* it's all right for me to speak now. Now that you've gone and told Jason *everything.*"

I gulped. Oh, no. She really was talking!

"Sure," said Coop. "Talk all you want, Lootna. We've got no secrets from Jason. He's part of the team now."

I was?

"And speaking of the team," Coop went on, "you might want to take a look at the spaceship, Jason. You can begin to get familiar with the controls and so forth. We should be leaving on our next mission in about, oh . . ."

He glanced at his watch.

". . . twelve minutes."

I felt my mouth drop open. "M-mission?" I managed to croak. "You've got a spaceship?"

"A two-man flyer," he said proudly. "Come on, I'll show you. It's in the garage."

He started toward the house—and I found myself following him. After all, he had a talking cat-creature for a pet, so he just might have a spaceship in his garage. I had to find out.

Lootna brought up the rear. "Well, I for one am *not* going," she announced as we went through the back door. "I've been on my last death-defying mission with you, Cooper Vor."

"You always say that, Lootna," said Coop cheerfully.

We walked through a perfectly ordinary kitchen. "Well, this time I mean it," said Lootna. "I've had enough excitement for one lifetime, thank you. Or maybe you've forgotten that on your last little mission my tail got crimped. Now *that* was fun."

"Now, Lootna," said Coop. "It was just a little crimp. And it looks fine now. Doesn't it, Jason?"

We were walking through a perfectly ordinary dining room. I stopped and looked at Lootna's tail. It was silky and black, with no bumps or bends in sight. "It looks great," I told her.

Lootna looked pleased. "Why, thank you," she said.

As we started down a perfectly ordinary hallway, Lootna walked beside me.

"Jason, you seem to be a sensible young man," she said. "So I'm going to give you some good advice. If I were you, I wouldn't touch this assistant job with a ten-foot pole."

"Oh?" I asked. "Why not?"

"Because Cooper here is always charging all over the galaxy, that's why," she said. "The ice moons of Argus, the lost colonies of the Larissa star system—you name it, he's been there. And no matter where he goes, he's always up to his ears in trouble."

"Trouble is my business," said Coop with a grin.

He had stopped by a door that looked like it might lead to his garage.

"Uh, what exactly *is* your business, Coop?" I asked.

"I'm a troubleshooter," he said. "An Intragalactic Troubleshooter. Best job there is. Suppose someone has a problem—anywhere in the galaxy. He hires me, and I zip right out and solve it for him. Any kind of problem. Big problems, little problems—"

"*Big* problems," Lootna put in. "They're always *big* problems. Problems that can get your tail crimped. Or worse."

Coop went right on. "I've tackled them all. Believe me, Jason, there's never a dull moment in this line of work. You're going to love it."

"But—"

Coop threw open the door.

"And you're going to love this, too," he added.

I peered into the garage. And caught my breath.

Wow! I thought.

There was nothing perfectly ordinary about *this*.

four

One look and I knew it wasn't from planet Earth.

It was a spaceship, all right. And it was built for speed.

It was long and gray and sleek—about the size of a speedboat. It had two short swept-back wings on the sides. Over the cockpit was a low transparent bubble. Even just sitting there, it looked *fast*.

But there was one thing I couldn't figure out. It was mounted on railroad tracks!

The spaceship was aimed toward the back of the garage, and the tracks ran right up to the back wall and stopped. Right there against the solid wall.

"I see you're wondering about the tracks," said Coop. "Well, see that wall?" He pointed to the back wall. "It's not really a wall. Here, get a load of this."

He pressed a button on his wristwatch.

Suddenly the whole wall just melted away. In its place was nothing but the color blue. Pure blue, from top to bottom. Like we were looking into a big patch of blue, blue sky.

"That's a wormhole into space," Coop explained. "Fly through there and you can pop out just about anywhere in the galaxy in a few seconds flat. If you know what you're doing, of course. Right, Lootna?"

Lootna jumped up onto the front of the spaceship. She began pacing back

and forth, swishing her long black tail.

"Oh, you know your way around a wormhole, all right," she said. "Just don't expect *me* to go with you, that's all. I've popped out in enough weird places with you, Cooper Vor. In other words, I've popped my last pop. I'm popped out. I'm pooped. So count me out. I'm not going."

Coop listened to her with a big grin on his face. "Whatever you say, Lootna," he said.

While they were talking, I kept glancing over at the huge square of blue. It was flat and deep at the same time. It was beautiful.

"Is that why you live here?" I asked Coop. "Because of the wormhole?"

"Right," he said. "You don't find them just anywhere, you know. There aren't any on my planet, for instance."

He glanced at his watch. "Oops. We'd better get a move on." He passed his hand over the bubble top and it swung open. "Hop in the other side, Jason. I'll tell you about our mission on the way."

He leaped into the spaceship and began fiddling with the controls.

I walked slowly around to the other side of the spaceship. This was it, I thought. Was I really going to go?

Being an assistant to an intragalactic troubleshooter did sound pretty exciting. And maybe I could make a little money, too. I mean, it was a real job and everything.

I thought about my other money-making project: being a door-to-door dog trainer. I thought about Ranger. Good old ankle-chewing Ranger. The dog with the brains of a Ping-Pong ball.

I decided to go with Coop.

"I have to be back in time for my drum lesson," I said as I climbed into the spaceship. "Will we be back by one o'clock?"

"With time to spare," said Coop.

He pressed several buttons on the computer panel in front of him. A strange, high-pitched sound came from somewhere in the spaceship.

Lootna was still sitting on the hood. "Forty seconds, Lootna," said Coop.

The sound got higher and higher until I couldn't hear it anymore. Straight ahead was the blue wormhole.

"Thirty seconds," said Coop.

Lootna didn't budge.

"Twenty seconds," said Coop.

"Well, I might just go along for the

ride," said Lootna. She jumped quickly into the spaceship behind Coop and me. "But if you think I'm getting involved in any mission, you're dreaming!"

Coop pressed another button, and the bubble over the cockpit swung closed. I held on to the arms of my seat. What was I doing? Where were we going? What was wrong with dog training anyway?

"Fifteen seconds," said Coop.

"I don't suppose I could ask where we're going," said Lootna.

"To the planet Urkar," said Coop. "Ten seconds."

"To the planet Urkar?" Lootna said slowly. "I seem to remember something about the planet Urkar." She paused a second and then said, "*Please* don't tell me that's Grugg the Awful's planet."

"It is," said Coop. "Five seconds."

Lootna groaned. She tapped me on the shoulder with her tail. "We're goners," she said.

"Blast off!" said Coop. He pushed a lever forward.

I was thrown back against the seat as the spaceship shot forward into the field of blue.

five

I couldn't believe it. A split second later we were skimming low over a dry desert planet!

We had to be going at least four hundred miles an hour, hugging the ground. Out ahead there was nothing but sand as far as the eye could see. Above us the sky was orange.

I held on tight as Coop banked the spaceship. We shot between two huge sand dunes and out over a sandy plain.

"Well, now," said Coop, "I think I'd better fill you two in on the mission before we get to the fortress."

"The fortress?" said Lootna. "Would that be Grugg the Awful's fortress? The fortress where we're all going to get thrown into the slime pit?"

"It's Grugg the Awful's fortress, all right," said Coop in high spirits. "But we're not going to get thrown into any slime pit. We're going to sneak in, get the energy crystal, and sneak out again. Nothing to it."

"Ha!" said Lootna.

"Uh, Coop," I said, "what energy crystal?"

"The one Grugg the Awful stole from the powerful Star King of Zarr," said Coop. "The Star King has hired us to get it back. It's a very special energy crystal. The only one of its kind."

Lootna sighed loudly. "And just what does this energy crystal do?" she asked.

"We might as well know what it does, since we're going to end up in the slime pit because of it."

"It's the power source for a robot," explained Coop. "A very famous robot. The Court Jester Robot of Zarr. The funniest robot in the galaxy."

Had I heard him right? "You mean it *tells jokes?*" I asked.

"Right," said Coop. "Hilarious jokes. I haven't heard it myself, but people say it's a ten-laugh-a-minute robot."

"I don't get it," I said. "How come Grugg the Awful stole the robot's energy crystal?"

"Because the robot made a big mistake," said Coop. "It told a joke about Grugg that Grugg didn't like."

Just then we came to a giant sand dune. It was as high as a skyscraper.

We whooshed up one side of it and zoomed down the other. My stomach was left up in the air.

"*Wheeeee!*" said Coop.

Lootna put her paw on my shoulder. "Can you believe it?" she said. "The captain of our spaceship just said, 'Wheeeee!' This is great. We're doomed."

I didn't know about that. But I did begin to wonder just how slimy the slime pit was.

A few minutes later Coop slowed the spaceship. He landed gently at the bottom of another large dune.

"Follow me," he said.

He jumped out and grabbed a silver bag from behind his seat. He went charging up the sand dune.

Lootna and I looked at each other. Then we both scrambled up after him.

When we got to the top, Coop was lying on his stomach. He was peering over the rim of the dune. Lootna and I crawled up next to him and peered over, too.

There it was. Grugg the Awful's fortress, surrounded by a sea of golden sand.

It was jet black—and as large as a small city. It had high thick walls, ugly square turrets, and a single huge gate. The moat around it was filled with some sort of oily black liquid. Over the gate were two huge crossed axes.

But the worst part was the creatures. Along the tops of the walls were a lot of very large creatures.

I swallowed hard.

"Hmmm," said Coop. "Just as I thought. Lots of guards."

"Lots of *large* guards," Lootna pointed

out. "They look like they weigh about two tons each. Let's just hope they don't decide to sit on us before they throw us into the slime pit."

"They'd have to catch us first," said Coop. He gave a confident grin. "But they won't. And I'll show you why."

He reached into the silver bag and pulled out three wide silver belts.

"Invisibility belts," he said. "One for each of us. We strap these belts on and become totally invisible. And then," he said, chuckling, "we waltz right into the fortress under their very noses."

six

Coop didn't waste any time. He strapped on one of the silver belts and pushed a button near the buckle.

Instantly he blinked out of sight. Gone. Without a trace.

I stared hard at where he'd been, but there was nothing there.

"Well?" came a voice from thin air. "How do I look?"

"Invisible," I said.

"Sort of invisible or very invisible?" he asked.

"Very invisible," I said.

"Perfect," he said. "Give yours a try."

He didn't have to ask me twice. I'd always wanted to be invisible. I buckled on one of the belts and pressed the button. For a second I noticed a fizzy feeling all over my body.

"Hmmm," said Lootna, looking surprised. "Yours works too, Jason. Amazing."

So I was invisible!

And now that I was, I could see Coop again! He was transparent and shimmery, but I could see him. I looked down at my own hand. It was transparent and shimmery, too.

Lootna held up the last belt with her tail. "Well, isn't anybody going to help me on with mine?" she said. She was trying to sound grumpy, but I could tell she really wanted to try that belt.

"Sure," said Coop. He wrapped the

belt three times around her middle. "I wasn't sure you were going along on the mission. I mean, you *said*—"

"You two are going to need all the help you can get," sniffed Lootna.

She looked down and admired herself in her belt. Then she reached up with her paw and pushed the button near her buckle. In a flash she turned shimmery, too.

"Okay, team," said Coop, "this is it. I know I don't have to remind you that this is a dangerous mission. We all know there's a slime pit in there with our name on it if we aren't careful. But it's up to us to put the Court Jester Robot of Zarr back into the joke business. So let's get in there and get that energy crystal."

"Right," said Lootna and I together. I think my voice squeaked a little, but nobody seemed to notice.

Then the three of us marched over the top of the sand dune and walked side by side toward the fortress.

The closer we got, the better we could see the guards. And the better we could see the guards, the harder my heart pounded. There were about fifty of them patrolling the tops of the walls. If we weren't invisible, then we were in big trouble.

These guys were giants. They were ten feet tall if they were an inch. They had huge bulging muscles and pink pig-like faces. They looked mean.

But they didn't see us. They just kept walking back and forth along the walls. So far, so good.

We reached the drawbridge that stretched across the moat. The black iron walls of the fortress loomed over us. At the other end of the drawbridge was the gate.

But we had a problem. Five guards were standing in front of the gate, talking.

I gulped.

They had beady orange eyes, and their huge piggish snouts wiggled around a lot when they talked. They wore shiny black uniforms with high collars—but no shoes. They had big hairy feet with three toes.

We began to tiptoe across the drawbridge toward them. Two of the guards were arguing. They were standing snout to snout, glaring at each other.

"You are sissy!" one of them was saying. "You afraid everything. You afraid snurk. You afraid itty-bitty snurk!"

"I afraid snurk?" growled the other guard. He gave a loud snort. "I no afraid snurk! I crunch snurk. I smash snurk. I eat snurk for breakfast."

"Haw-haw," said the first guard. "You make laugh. You afraid snurk. You afraid teeny-weeny snurk."

"How you like snout bashed, flappy mouth?"

"Who do this? You not big enough, short stuff."

"Oh, this good! Now I short stuff! You put up fists."

Coop signaled for Lootna and me to try to get by. Right away Lootna spotted an opening between two of the guards. She put her ears down and darted through.

"Ha!" the first guard was saying. "Here my fists. Now I conk head. Make

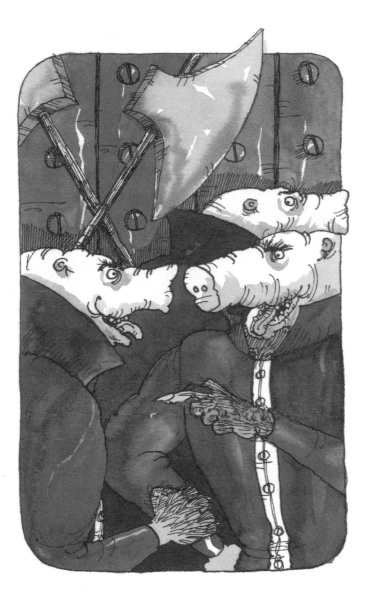

head flat. How you like?"

"Big talk, big snout."

"Who you call big snout?"

I tiptoed around to the left—but was blocked. Then I circled to the right and squeezed around on the outside. One of the guards almost backed into me as I slipped by.

Whew! Lootna and I had made it. We looked back at Coop.

I couldn't believe my eyes. Coop was right in the middle of the guards, kneeling down. There was a big grin on his face. He was tickling one of the guards' toes!

It was the tough-talking guard who had started the argument. He gave a surprised snort and kicked his foot in the air.

"EEEEEE!" he yelled. "What *that?*"

Coop tickled his other foot.

"YAAA!" yelled the guard. "SNURK! SNURK ON FOOT!" He began hopping from foot to foot, swatting at his feet and kicking wildly.

The other guards burst into loud laughter. They snorted and grunted and hooted and howled. I'd never heard so much racket. It sounded like a couple of hundred pigs in hog heaven.

"Hee-hee, you funny!" cried one of them.

"Dance good! Dance funny!" cried another.

Suddenly Coop tickled the toes of the other four guards. They all began hopping around and whacking at their feet.

"AAAAAAAA!" yelled one.

"SNURK!" yelled another.

"HELP!" yelled another.

Coop came diving out from the middle of them. He hurried past Lootna and me, taking giant tiptoe steps. "Is this fun, or what?" he whispered as he went by.

I looked at Lootna. She rolled her eyes and sighed with disgust.

"What did I tell you?" she whispered. "The man is hopeless."

Then the two of us tiptoed after Coop into the gloomy halls of the fortress.

seven

Coop checked the direction finder on his watch. "This way," he whispered.

We sneaked down a long hallway. Every now and then Coop checked his direction finder again. It was locked in on the stolen energy crystal.

We turned left down another hallway. Then right. Then left again. The fortress was like a giant maze.

Guards were everywhere. The halls echoed with their grunting and snorting. Whenever a group of them marched toward us, we flattened ourselves against the walls to let them by. Their long toenails went *scratch! scratch! scratch!* on the stone floor as they passed.

Finally we came to a huge open doorway. Two guards stood at attention on either side of it.

Coop pointed to the doorway. "It's in there somewhere," he whispered to Lootna and me.

The three of us tiptoed in. Then we just stood there, staring.

Uh-oh, I thought. Trouble.

We were in an enormous room, filled with maybe two hundred soldiers and guards. Most of them were facing the far end of the room, where a huge black iron throne stood in the middle of a raised platform.

On the throne sat Grugg. Grugg the Awful himself. I could tell it was him because he lived up to his name.

He was like the others, but much worse. Much bigger, much uglier, and much meaner-looking. He had muscles like watermelons, and a snout that would've put a prize porker to shame. He was wearing a shiny black hat with a pair of crossed axes painted on it.

Suddenly I noticed something else. Grugg's hairy feet were resting on a large glass box. Inside the box was a sparkling green crystal.

I knew right away what it was: the stolen energy crystal.

Coop signaled to Lootna and me, and the three of us put our heads together in a huddle.

"All right, team," whispered Coop, "no use dallying around. Let's get that crystal. We'll split into two groups. I'll try to find a way to get Grugg's ugly

feet off that glass box. If I do, you two grab the crystal."

Before Lootna or I could say a word, Coop was sneaking away toward a large group of guards.

We stared after him. Why was he going that way, *away* from Grugg?

But there was no time to worry about Coop. Lootna and I had a job to do. We slipped through the crowd to the front of the room. We climbed onto the platform and stationed ourselves on either side of the glass box . . . and Grugg the Awful's feet. Then we waited.

Grugg loomed over us like a huge hoggish mountain. He drummed his fingers on the armrest of the throne as he scowled out over the room. His orange eyes glittered.

Suddenly, his voice boomed out.

"Commander of North! Where Commander of North?"

"Here, sir!" came a voice from the crowd.

"How things in North?" demanded Grugg.

"Good, sir! Things go good in North!"

"Commander of South!" bellowed Grugg. "How things in South?"

"Good, sir! No could be better!" called out another voice.

"Commander of East!" roared Grugg. "How things in East?"

"What's it to you, fathead?" yelled Coop from somewhere in the crowd.

Grugg the Awful looked like he was going to swallow his teeth. He sprang to his feet.

"Who say that?" he thundered.

"That's for me to know and you to

find out, blubber brain!" yelled Coop.

Grugg charged over to the edge of the platform and leaped off into the crowd. "Me find!" he roared. "Break bones! Throw in slime pit!"

Lootna and I moved fast. Lootna flipped open the lid of the glass box. I reached in, grabbed the crystal, and stuffed it into my pocket. Once inside my pocket, the crystal was invisible too. Lootna lowered the lid.

Mission accomplished! We headed for the door on the double.

We were almost there when we spotted Coop sneaking out of the crowd. He was heading for the door, too.

But something was wrong.

First he was shimmery, then he was solid. Then shimmery, then solid. His invisibility belt was failing!

I saw him glance down at his body. "Oops," I heard him say. "Should've charged those batteries a little longer."

By now he was completely visible. He made a break for the door.

Too late.

"Seize him!" roared Grugg, pointing from across the room.

Two huge guards grabbed hold of Coop and lifted him off his feet.

eight

Grugg the Awful rushed across the room and scowled down at Coop.

"Who you?" he demanded.

Coop cleared his throat. The two guards were holding him up by his arms. His feet were dangling a few inches above the floor. I could tell he was thinking hard.

"Me?" he said. "You kidding? You not know? Me new cook! Just arrive today. Where kitchen? Me go now. Cook Grugg good dinner! Cook deep-dish combination pizza. Plenty pepperoni, onions, mushrooms. Extra cheese. But no worry, no put anchovies. You like! Me go now."

Grugg didn't buy it.

"You lie! You no cook!" he roared. "You go slime pit!"

He gestured to the guards who were holding Coop. They started to carry him out.

"Wait!" said Coop. "Let's talk this over!"

Grugg gestured to the guards again. They put Coop down and shoved him forward.

"Good!" grunted Grugg. "Ears ready. You talk. Who you?"

Coop shifted his weight. "Ahem. Yes, well, uh . . ." His voice trailed off as he tried to think of something.

Suddenly, I got an idea. But how could I tell Coop about it without the guards hearing me?

I thought of a way. Quickly I sneaked around behind Coop. Then I jumped up, grabbed his shoulders, and pulled myself up close to his ear.

"Coop!" I whispered. "Tell him you're a powerful magician."

Coop didn't blink an eye. "Since you insist, Grugg," he said in a loud voice, "I shall tell you who I am. I'm a magician! The most powerful magician in the galaxy! Warriors and kings tremble before me!"

"Tell him," I whispered, "that he'd better let you go or you'll turn his snout green."

"And I suggest you let me go at once," Coop warned, "or I'll turn your miserable snout green! A *disgusting* color of green. And I'll sprinkle it with purple warts, too!"

Grugg the Awful snorted. He still looked ferocious, but he was beginning to look a little worried, too.

"You magician?" he grunted. "You no magician. Grugg no believe. Grugg no fool."

"Tell him," I whispered, "that you'll prove you're a magician. You'll make things rise into the air and float around the room. Lootna and I will make it happen."

"You don't believe me?" Coop boomed at Grugg. "You doubt my word? Then behold! I shall demonstrate my fantastic powers!"

I let go of Coop's shoulders and dropped to the floor. Then I hurried over to Lootna and filled her in on the plan. "Good thinking, Jason," she whispered.

"That bowl!" Coop cried out. He

65

pointed across the room. "Does everybody see that bowl?"

All eyes turned toward the other side of the room. In the middle of a long table was a big wooden bowl, surrounded by a bunch of wooden cups.

"At my command," Coop announced, "that bowl will rise into the air!"

"I'll handle this one," I whispered to Lootna. I sneaked quickly across the room and stood next to the bowl.

Phew! Ick! Whatever was in that bowl was pretty stinky. I peeked in. *Yugh!* It was some sort of thick, muddy-looking liquid with soggy yellow leaves floating in it. Did these guys actually drink this stuff? I wondered.

"Rise, bowl!" cried Coop. "Rise!" He raised his hands slowly as if he were lifting the bowl.

I cupped my hands under the bowl and slowly lifted it up. Of course, to everyone else it looked like the bowl was floating in thin air. Snorts and gasps of surprise filled the room.

I had to gasp myself—from the smell. *Yecchh!* I thought. What *is* this gunk, anyway?

"What is in the bowl?" Coop asked Grugg.

"Soup," grunted Grugg. "Spluggard soup. Good. Much good. Put hair on chest."

I didn't want to know what a spluggard was. I already knew how it smelled. I held the bowl out at arm's length. *Gag!*

"I shall drink that spluggard soup!" said Coop.

What?!!! I thought.

"I shall drink that spluggard soup

without moving from this spot!" he said. "I shall drink it from all the way across the room!"

Coop's hands were still raised in front of him. Now he opened his mouth and began tilting his hands up, as if he were pouring the soup down his throat.

Oh, no! I tilted the bowl and began drinking. What else could I do? *Aggh! Igg! Retch! Bleccch!*

Coop tilted his hands back down. So did I. I think my eyes were crossed.

"Yummy!" Coop exclaimed, smacking his lips. "Delicious! This spluggard soup is superb!"

Ack!

"I do believe I'll have some more!" said Coop.

Ack!

We drank again—Coop pretending,

me for real. A big slimy leaf slid into my mouth. I swallowed it whole and kept on drinking. *Blugggggh!*

"Ahhhh!" said Coop, lowering his hands. "Now *that* was refreshing!"

I put the bowl down. Then I leaned against the table for support. I didn't know if spluggard soup was going to put any hair on my chest, but I was pretty sure it was going to put hair on my tongue.

Grugg the Awful and his men were staring at Coop. They looked amazed. Coop took out a handkerchief and dabbed his lips.

"And now," he declared, "I shall perform my second demonstration!"

What? I thought. Another one? Wasn't one enough? Wasn't one *more* than enough? I burped.

"Watch closely, Grugg," Coop went on, "for I shall now make your hat rise from your head and fly about the room!"

Good grief, I thought. I looked at Lootna. How were we going to do that? Grugg was ten feet tall. I could never reach his hat, and neither could Lootna.

"In exactly fifteen seconds," said Coop, "your hat will leap from your head! Fourteen . . . thirteen . . . twelve . . ."

Lootna suddenly ran over near Grugg. She signaled me with her tail to come over and stand next to her. I did. Then she backed away a short distance and came racing toward me.

"Four . . . three . . . two . . ."

Lootna leaped into the air, sprang off the top of my shoulder, and sailed up and over Grugg's head. She snatched his hat with her teeth as she went by.

71

She was great. She landed without a sound.

"Now, fly, hat! Fly!" cried Coop. He pointed to a far corner of the room. "Over there!"

I knew what I had to do. I raced toward the corner. About a gallon of spluggard soup sloshed around in my stomach. Lootna flipped Grugg's hat from her mouth back to her tail. Then she gave it a powerful toss, throwing it like a Frisbee. I arrived just in time to catch it on the fly.

"Now over there!" cried Coop, pointing.

I gave the hat a backhanded flip and sent it sailing. A bunch of guards snorted with fear and dived out of the way. Lootna streaked across the room, leaped, and snatched the hat out of the air.

"Now over there!" cried Coop.

Lootna fired the hat. I sprinted over and caught it.

"Now out the window!" cried Coop.

Wait a minute, I thought. Out the window? Is that a good idea?

"Now out the window!" Coop cried again.

I threw the hat out the window.

"GROINK?" said Grugg.

nine

There was a shocked silence.

Grugg just stood there, staring out the window after his hat.

Had Coop gone too far?

One of the guards leaned out the window and looked down. "Hat in moat," he grunted. He kept on looking down. After a minute he added, "Hat sinking."

Grugg shifted his beady orange eyes to Coop. His snout was twitching.

I held my breath.

Suddenly, Grugg gave a loud grunt. *"Release magician!"* he ordered with a wave of his hand. *"Magician free."*

We did it! Coop was free! Lootna and I started for the door. Let's get out of here while the getting is good, I said to myself.

But Coop wasn't ready to go. He was enjoying himself too much.

"A wise decision, Grugg, old boy," he was saying. "You have saved your snout from a terrible fate this day. Green is an awful color for a snout. And purple is an awful color for warts, too."

Lootna stopped and rolled her eyes.

"Yes," Coop went on, "you will not regret this decision, Grugg, my friend. True, you have lost a hat. And a fine hat it was, too. But—"

Lootna trotted over and bit Coop on the ankle.

"I'll be going now," said Coop.

He turned and came striding toward

the door. Grugg scowled after him. His snout was still twitching.

Coop, Lootna, and I went out and headed down the hallway. Once Coop got moving, he didn't fool around. Lootna and I had to trot alongside him to keep up.

We retraced our steps through the fortress. Right, then left, then right again. We came to the gate and crossed the drawbridge. We started out across the sand.

And that's when I felt a fizzy feeling.

I looked down at myself. I was flickering! I looked over at Lootna. She was flickering, too!

Our invisibility belts were failing!

"Run!" yelled Coop. We broke into a run.

"Three!" came a cry from behind us.

"Now are three of them!"

I glanced back over my shoulder. Suddenly Grugg the Awful appeared on top of the wall. "ENERGY CRYSTAL MISSING!" he thundered. "GET! CATCH!"

We ran for our lives. Grugg's men came pouring out of the fortress. They pounded across the drawbridge after us.

We reached the sand dune and started scrambling up. There was a lot of angry *groink-groink-groink*ing behind us—and it was getting closer fast.

We got to the top of the dune and flung ourselves down the other side. We went leaping, sliding, bounding down the soft sand. I tripped and began to roll. I caught a glimpse back up the dune.

They were coming over the top!

Thud! I rolled into the side of the spaceship. I jumped to my feet. Coop

was vaulting into the cockpit. Lootna was already inside. I leaped in beside them.

As Coop slammed the bubble top closed, I looked out. About a hundred huge bodies were tumbling and rolling down the dune toward us. It seemed to be raining giant hogs.

"GROINK! GROINK! GROINK! GROINK!"

Coop jammed the lever forward.

We left Grugg the Awful's men in our dust.

ten

"Piece of cake," said Coop, grinning a big grin.

"We're alive! We're alive!" said Lootna, grinning a big grin.

"I'll never complain about eating liver again," I said, burping.

We were speeding over the sandy plain, back toward the wormhole we'd come through.

"Let's see that energy crystal again," said Coop.

I held it up. It sparkled like a green jewel.

Coop grinned some more. "Are we a

great team, or what?" he said. "By the way, that was quick thinking back there, Jason. Your idea about me being a magician, I mean. If it weren't for you, I'd be in the slime pit right now."

"Probably would've done you some good," said Lootna. Then she patted me on the shoulder with her paw. "But it's nice to know *somebody* around here has some sense."

I didn't know quite what to say. "Er, thanks," I said.

"Setting a course for Zarr," said Coop. "We'll just pop by and deliver this crystal to the Star King before we head back to Earth."

That sounded good to me. It might give us a chance to see the Court Jester Robot of Zarr. The funniest robot in the galaxy.

The wormhole appeared up ahead. It looked like a square of blue floating against the orange sky. "This will be a little side trip of about sixty trillion miles," Coop said as we zoomed into it.

A split second later we zoomed out another wormhole. This one was inside an enormous cavern. The spaceship swooped to a stop.

We climbed out.

After a minute a door opened at the far end of the cavern, and a tall man in a blue robe hurried toward us. His pale-white skin glowed. Behind him two furry buck-toothed creatures were struggling to carry a little robot about my size.

"Cooper Vor!" the Star King burst out. "You got it! You got it! Tell me you got it!"

"We got it," said Coop. I handed Coop the energy crystal, and he held it up. "Couldn't have done it without Lootna and my Earthling friend here."

The Star King thanked Coop and Lootna and me again and again. Meanwhile, the buck-toothed creatures staggered over beside him and set the robot down on its feet.

I have to admit the Court Jester Robot didn't look like I'd imagined. It had striped metal legs, rosy cheeks painted on its metal face, and a pointy head with a bell on top.

"I only hope the crystal hasn't been damaged," said the Star King as Coop handed it to him. "Things have been pretty dull around here without a few good jokes to lighten things up."

He didn't have to worry. The crystal

worked. As soon as it was plugged into the robot's chest, the robot's eyes lit up.

It looked around. It saw Lootna.

"Wow!" it said. "Now *those* are ears. Your brain must be just one big muscle to hold up those whoppers!"

The bell on its head jingled, and the robot broke into snickers. "Ho, ho. Just kidding," it went on. "But seriously, are those really ears, or is that the silliest hat in the galaxy?"

The bell rang again and the robot laughed like a loon. Lootna glared at it through narrowed eyes.

"Whoooeeee!" crowed the robot. "Am I funny, or am I funny?"

Actually, I had my doubts, but the Star King didn't. He was holding his sides and chuckling away.

The robot leaned toward Lootna and

nudged her with his elbow. "Well, how about it, beautiful? How about giving me a big round of applause with those ears?"

Then it hooted with laughter. So did the Star King.

"How would you like a knuckle sandwich instead?" snapped Lootna.

"Oh, so you want to fight, do you?" said the Court Jester Robot. It put up its fists and began dancing around like a boxer. "Okay, sure, I'll fight, I'll fight. But first you have to tie one of those ears behind your back!"

The bell went wild and the robot doubled over with laughter. The Star King hee-hee-heed until his eyes watered.

"I'm so *funny!*" gasped the robot.

Lootna snorted with disgust. "I *think*," she said with dignity, "that I have better things to do than listen to *this*."

She stalked off toward the spaceship.

The Star King gave a few more chuckles and then wiped his eyes. "A good laugh is worth its weight in gold," he said. "Which reminds me. Here comes your payment, Cooper."

The two furry creatures had returned, each lugging a large metal can. They carried the cans over to the spaceship and put them in behind Coop's seat, next to Lootna.

"It's paint," said the Star King. "But not ordinary paint. It's called Startint, and it's worth a fortune. I'aint your spaceship with it, and the spaceship will change color to match its surroundings. It's the best camouflage in the galaxy."

Coop looked impressed. "Terrific," he said. "In our line of work, you need all the camouflage you can get."

Coop and I said good-bye to the Star King and climbed into the spaceship. Just before the bubble top snapped closed, the robot cupped its hands around its mouth.

"Hey, cat!" it called to Lootna. "Take my advice. You've just *got* to lay off those ear-stretching exercises!"

"Oh, brother," muttered Lootna.

And the last thing I saw on Zarr was the Star King and the Court Jester Robot collapsing against each other in laughter.

eleven

A half hour later I was walking down the sidewalk toward home, humming to myself.

I felt good. I felt great. Coop had asked me to be a permanent member of the team, so I was now an official Intragalactic Troubleshooter!

I sneaked another look at my communicator watch. Coop had given it to me as soon as we got back to Earth. It looked like an ordinary watch, but actually it was a two-way viewing screen. Coop said that whenever he needed to contact me about a mission, he'd call me up on my watch. It could do all sorts of other neat things, too. It had a siren. And a laser. And an emergency signal light.

Suddenly, the communicator gave a bleep.

The watch face faded out, and in came Coop's face in full color.

"Testing, testing," he said. "Are you there, Jason?"

I looked around to be sure no one was watching me. Then I pushed a button on my watch. "Right here," I said.

"Hey, it works," said Coop, looking pretty happy about it. "Okay, listen. I just thought you'd like to know that we may have another mission lined up. Have you ever heard of the Zeek star system?"

Lootna squeezed into the corner of the screen. "Yes, and have you ever heard of the *Lizard Pirates* of Zeek?" she asked.

"The *giant* Lizard Pirates of Zeek? With teeth like knives? Trust me, Jason. Take a rain check on this one. That's what *I'm* doing. I'm not about to—"

"Now, Lootna," said Coop, "we can discuss the details with Jason tomorrow. He has a drum lesson to get to right now." Then he added to me, "Can you be here about eleven in the morning?"

"Uh, sure," I said.

Lizard Pirates? I was thinking. Teeth like *knives*?

"Great," said Coop. "Over and out."

And then, just before he faded from the screen, he grinned and added, "Didn't I tell you you were going to love this business?"